THE TAILOR OF GLOSTER

SQUIRREL NUTKIN

NUTS

TOM KITTEN

PETER RABBIT

D0959801

Frederick Warne has a continuing commitment to reproduce Beatrix Potter's exquisite watercolours to the highest possible standard. In 1993 and 1994, taking advantage of the latest advances in printing technology and expertise, entirely new film was made from her original book illustrations. The drawings are now reproduced with a quality and a degree of authenticity never before attainable in print.

FREDERICK WARNE

Published by the Penguin Group
27 Wrights Lane, London W8 5TZ, England
Penguin Books USA Inc., 375 Hudson Street, New York, N.Y. 10014, USA
Penguin Books Australia Ltd, Ringwood, Victoria, Australia
Penguin Books Canada Ltd, 10 Alcorn Avenue, Toronto, Ontario, Canada M4V 3B2
Penguin Books (N.Z.) Ltd, 182-190 Wairau Road, Auckland 10, New Zealand

Penguin Books Ltd, Registered Offices: Harmondsworth, Middlesex, England

First published 1902 by Frederick Warne
This edition with new reproductions of Beatrix Potter's book illustrations first
published 1996

Colour reproduction by
Saxon Photolitho Ltd, Norwich
Printed and bound in Great Britain by
William Clowes Limited, Beccles and London

THE TALE OF
PETER RABBIT

❀

BY BEATRIX POTTER

F. WARNE & Co

ONCE upon a time there were four little Rabbits, and their names were—Flopsy, Mopsy, Cotton-tail, and Peter.

They lived with their Mother in a sand-bank, underneath the root of a very big fir-tree.

"NOW, my dears," said old Mrs. Rabbit one morning, "you may go into the fields or down the lane, but don't go into Mr. McGregor's garden: your Father had an accident there; he was put in a pie by Mrs. McGregor."

"NOW run along, and don't get into mischief. I am going out."

Then old Mrs. Rabbit took a basket and her umbrella, and went through the wood to the baker's. She bought a loaf of brown bread and five currant buns.

FLOPSY, Mopsy, and Cotton-tail, who were good little bunnies, went down the lane to gather blackberries.

BUT Peter, who was very naughty, ran
straight away to Mr. McGregor's garden, and
squeezed under the gate!

FIRST he ate some lettuces and some French beans; and then he ate some radishes.

AND then, feeling rather sick, he went to look for some parsley.

BUT round the end of a cucumber frame, whom should he meet but Mr. McGregor!

Mr. McGregor was on his hands and knees planting out young cabbages, but he jumped up and ran after Peter, waving a rake and calling out, "Stop thief!"

PETER was most dreadfully frightened; he rushed all over the garden, for he had forgotten the way back to the gate.

He lost one of his shoes among the cabbages, and the other shoe amongst the potatoes.

AFTER losing them, he ran on four legs and went faster, so that I think he might have got away altogether if he had not unfortunately run into a gooseberry net, and got caught by the large buttons on his jacket. It was a blue jacket with brass buttons, quite new.

PETER gave himself up for lost, and shed big
tears; but his sobs were overheard by some
friendly sparrows, who flew to him in great
excitement, and implored him to exert himself.

MR. McGREGOR came up with a sieve,
which he intended to pop upon the top of
Peter; but Peter wriggled out just in time,
leaving his jacket behind him.

A ND rushed into the tool-shed, and jumped into a can. It would have been a beautiful thing to hide in, if it had not had so much water in it.

Mr. McGregor was quite sure that Peter was somewhere in the tool-shed, perhaps hidden underneath a flower-pot. He began to turn them over carefully, looking under each.

Presently Peter sneezed—"Kertyschoo!" Mr. McGregor was after him in no time.

AND tried to put his foot upon Peter, who jumped out of a window, upsetting three plants. The window was too small for Mr. McGregor, and he was tired of running after Peter. He went back to his work.

PETER sat down to rest; he was out of breath and trembling with fright, and he had not the least idea which way to go. Also he was very damp with sitting in that can.

After a time he began to wander about, going lippity—lippity—not very fast, and looking all round.

HE found a door in a wall; but it was locked, and there was no room for a fat little rabbit to squeeze underneath.

An old mouse was running in and out over the stone door-step, carrying peas and beans to her family in the wood.

Peter asked her the way to the gate, but she had such a large pea in her mouth that she could not answer. She only shook her head at him. Peter began to cry.

THEN he tried to find his way straight across the garden, but he became more and more puzzled. Presently, he came to a pond where Mr. McGregor filled his water-cans.

A white cat was staring at some gold-fish; she sat very, very still, but now and then the tip of her tail twitched as if it were alive. Peter thought it best to go away without speaking to her; he had heard about cats from his cousin, little Benjamin Bunny.

HE went back towards the tool-shed, but suddenly, quite close to him, he heard the noise of a hoe—scr-r-ritch, scratch, scratch, scritch. Peter scuttered underneath the bushes. But presently, as nothing happened, he came out, and climbed upon a wheelbarrow and peeped over. The first thing he saw was Mr. McGregor hoeing onions. His back was

turned towards Peter, and beyond him was the gate!

Peter got down very quietly off the wheelbarrow, and started running as fast as he could go, along a straight walk behind some black-currant bushes.

MR. McGREGOR caught sight of him at the corner, but Peter did not care. He slipped underneath the gate, and was safe at last in the wood outside the garden.

MR. McGREGOR hung up the little jacket and the shoes for a scare-crow to frighten the blackbirds.

PETER never stopped running or looked
behind him till he got home to the big fir-tree.

He was so tired that he flopped down upon
the nice soft sand on the floor of the rabbit-
hole and shut his eyes. His mother was busy
cooking; she
wondered what
he had done
with his
clothes. It
was the
second little
jacket and
pair of shoes
that Peter
had lost in a
fortnight!

I AM sorry to say that Peter was not very well during the evening.

His mother put him to bed, and made some camomile tea; and she gave a dose of it to Peter!

"One table-spoonful to be taken at bed-time."

BUT Flopsy, Mopsy, and Cotton-tail had bread and milk and blackberries for supper.

THE END